# Hers

## is

## Beauty

by: Brandon Boyd

"Hers is Beauty," by Brandon Boyd. ISBN 1-58939-311-2.

Published 2002 by Virtualbookworm.com Publishing Inc., P.O. Box 9949, College Station, TX , 77842, US. ©2002 Brandon Boyd. All rights reserved. No part of this publication may be reproduced, stored in a retrieval system, or transmitted in any form or by any means, electronic, mechanical, recording or otherwise, without the prior written permission of Brandon Boyd.

Manufactured in the United States of America

_____ *A Heart's Gratitude* _____

*Dear God:*

*You are my all.*

_____ Dedication _____

Mom, thank you for teaching me what it truly means to have the heart of a gentleman.

# Introduction

This is my heart.

As I sit along the shoreline taking hold of the serenity of a distant sunrise, my heart is forever soaring with hers.
Without the slightest hesitation, I realize that a tiny
grain of sand is like the essence of a woman.
Until you take the time to appreciate its uniqueness, what you hold in the stillness of your hand will always be simply a grain of sand.

*A closed heart will never know of sorrow, yet neither will it ever know of love.*

*It is only right that she is never left without true happiness.*

As I whisper into her ear words that I have
longed to say,
speaking to the very openness
of her heart, ever so soft spoken I give
her this most pleasant compliment: the
sweetest fragrance of a woman is not
her perfume, it's her scent.

Four

*Kind words that are often
spoken can never go unheard.*

*Her encouragement is present in every single moment.*

_____ Six _____

As I hold with all care the
warmth of her hand, yet touching the
smoothness of her face,
in such a defining moment
our hearts slowly begin to meet. On this
night filled with a most certain charm,
I share with her what she has always
missed: finally fulfilling her expectations
of a little kiss.

_____ Seven _____

*Sincerity is not the measure of
the act but of the heart's intentions.*

*She is to ❀ be cherished.*

As I watch her sleep in
the comfort of my arms,
I am falling for her all over again.
In the calmness of this silent night,
I cry her tears, tears
that her heart has so many times shown,
yet in this most deserving moment of love I
promise that I will forever take her every

tear as my very own.

_____ Ten _____

*Love is the beauty of what is seen, yet sometimes it speaks of that which goes unrecognized.*

_____ *Eleven*_____

*Her sensitivity is unbelievable, yet so true.*

_____ *Twelve* _____

As I listen to the wonderful thoughts
of her heart expressed through the delicateness
of her voice, face to face I make a
tender promise that this cherished woman,
whom I so much adore, will always have
a hand to hold and a grateful heart which
will always be spoken for.

_____ Thirteen _____

*A heart that bares an imprint
of love is one that has undeniably
been forever touched.*

In all of ✿ her gracefulness,
She is woman, She is beauty.

As I hold her favorite teddy bear close
to the fondness of my heart, in my
mind I reminisce about all the
delightfulness that love can bring, for what is so
sweet and
yet so subtle are those timely moments
when a unexpected hug turns into a cozy
cuddle.

_____ Sixteen _____

*Love should be evident in all that truly defines the involvement of two hearts.*

_____ *Seventeen* _____

*Without question, she is the answer to a heart's every prayer.*

_____ *Eighteen* _____

As I carry her in the strength of my arms
while much needed raindrops freely fall,
in the midst of this enchanting moment
I know that
in the harmony of two, love
is as the steady waters, our hearts its
most precious seed.

_____ *Nineteen* _____

*If two hearts can love knowing what it means to grow, than they can grow knowing what it means to love.*

_____ Twenty _____

*She will always be the one as long as she remains second to none.*

_____ Twenty-one _____

As I continue to discover more about her as a woman, I am in love with her like no other before. For the very first time the abundance of my heart can feel what the sparkle in my eyes can see. She truly is in all her passion far more magnificent than I ever hoped her to be.

*At first glance love can appear to be hidden, yet in seeing the whole picture its true influence cannot be ignored.*

She is to ❀ be appreciated.

As I am reminded of a simple story once told, she
is the embodiment of everything in love that I need,
in all life's lessons I
have come to see: two people can't
experience the richness of a happy ending until
not only their eyes but their hearts learn
to be still.

*A heart with patience knows of
all the amazing gifts that lie in waiting.*

*Her strength defines all that she is.*

_____ *Twenty-seven* _____

As I take a familiar stroll through
the park drawing near to the affirmation
of her love, I have this
unrehearsed thought: if the origin of a
woman's beauty were to be traced:
present is her heart, absent is her face.

*In truth is where two hearts in agreement lie.*

*In all of* ❀ *her purpose,*
*She is woman, She is beauty.*

_____ *Thirty*_____

As I look at her blossoming as a fragile
flower early in the Springtime, in
the timelessness of every moment I know
that in all ways love is the reason why
given unto every heart is the beauty of its
own season.

*Given its good qualities, love should always be taken to heart.*

*In her, I have found that her genuineness is never lost on me.*

Thirty-three

As I admire the breathtaking beauty of her picture resting upon my nightstand, a simple teardrop begins to stream down my face. It is apparent that I have forever captured an intimate glimpse of her heart's portrait. Such endearing moments I will never forget.

_____ Thirty-four _____

*Love is as a reflection holding*
*all things envisioned in the mind to be seen, yet it's as*
*a little impression leaving all things caressed in the*
*heart*
*to be remembered.*

_____ *Thirty-five*_____

*She always remembers to never forget the sounds of laughter.*

As I walk beside her hand and hand on life's
journey, I am forever upholding her
as the candlelight of my
love. In all honesty I offer her this
much in the lasting memories of togetherness, in
the promises of a heart's touch.

_____ Thirty-seven _____

*Love is held in the highest regard to a person whose heart has yet to be touched and yet is not untouchable.*

Thirty-eight

*She is to ❀ be understood.*

As I offer forth my hand in
unending love with her standing
in her flowing white dress here by my side,
I am so glad for we are a match made in Heaven.
In something so uplifting I realize
that a wife, will become of this woman whom I will
forever see as my most
beloved bride.

_____ Forty _____

*One of the most enduring works of love is its ability to draw two hearts unto itself.*

*She is all that she is, by design.*

As I lie awake thinking about her
flourishing, in every breath of my
my heart lies reflections of those picturesque
nights when I glanced out of my window
and in a distance I could see her just before
she fell silently to sleep. Then I thought--
"Lord, give her a gentle hug for me."

_____ Forty-three _____

A heart that is thankful can see
something so little, yet let so much
of its virtue be seen.

*In all of ❀ her inspiration,*
*She is woman, She is beauty.*

As I blow a kiss into the many
ways of the wind, it carries forth the
signature of my love into her heart. It
speaks of her as a jewel even in silence,
for in such clarity it is obvious that this is about
allowing our
hearts to feel that which is so moving,
that which is most real.

_____ Forty-six _____

*For love to be real is perhaps the greatest realization of a heart's dream.*

*Her tears are shared in every way.*

As I sit in front of a campfire
gazing up at the twinkling starlight,
I notice a breeze ever so gentle in its
movement. It abides in the
flawlessness of
the night. It will always remind me
that in the
bond of companionship, what
is most dear is in those quiet moments
when no words are spoken, love's meaning
becomes so clear.

_____ Forty-nine _____

*A relationship holds no meaning*
*if love has yet to be defined.*

*Her compassion reaffirms her true nature.*

As I present to her the keepsake of my heart, it
speaks ever so fluently
of her giftedness in the language of love.
At such the right time I have decided,
I hope that she will always feel welcome--
all her wonderfulness is forever invited.


_____ *Fifty-two* _____

*A heart's most well written invitation is for another to share in the company of its love.*

She is to ❀ be held.

As I describe to her wholeheartedly what she truly
means to me, I will
forever believe that with her endless
love I've found that significant other I've
always wanted to meet--a lovely lady in
all her ways complete.

Love is easily relatable between

two hearts that have its

beauty in

common.

*In every telling moment nothing felt in the heart goes untold.*

As I sit in a cozy little coffeehouse
in the heart of the city, my feelings are of
happiness. These feelings arise from a time
that continues to bare witness to the growth
in our lives. I find satisfaction in that
whether it is in the serenity of night or the joy
of day, our love is the beauty of what we do and
the fulfillment of what we say.

*A heart's true complexion is most revealed when its love for another is not without demonstration.*

In all of ❀ her commitment,
She is woman, She is beauty.

_____ Sixty _____

As I stand out on an old wooden pier
embracing the dawning of nightfall,
waiting patiently in the distance I
glance over into the innocence of her eyes.
In such a picture perfect moment
I know that sometimes in the subtleness of
love the sun must momentarily set if in all
its beauty it is forever to arise.

*An apology is an expression of what
a heart has done, but in such a simple
act forgiven is what that heart will
become.*

*Her courage is known when it is most needed.*

As I serenade her heart with a
self -written lullaby, its words hold the truth of her

ways as a woman.

With her in mind , I am reassured that in all

that changes what will forever remain the same is

that in my eyes beauty will always be her

name.

*Of all things considered priceless,*
*love comes to mind when it has been*
*brought to heart.*

Sixty-five

*Her words are her most treasured possession.*

Sixty-six

As I glance down at a hidden river, I hold a unseen reflection of her in my heart. These memorable moments illustrate that sometimes a heart's hope-filled search for another is like a little flower petal flowing down stream, for no matter how far it gets it is never as far as it may seem.

Sometimes the measure of strength
is not so much in letting go of what
we can see as it is in holding onto the beauty
of that which does not yet exist.

Sixty-eight

*She is to ❀ be respected.*

As I express the innermost feelings
of admiration known by my heart, it
is the undeniable elegance that I see
in her as a woman that my mind cannot
erase. In such appreciation I will always
love her, not only for her kindness but
especially for her grace.

_____ Seventy _____

*A heart that can love in humility
will always find happiness to be
within its midst.*

Her gentleness is as a little feather
blowing in the wind.

As I dwell on her unforgettable presence,
I vividly recall how she was mine at first sight. In
the very depths
of my heart I am speechless for I have come to
believe
that sharing is not only how we give,
but also how we receive.

_____ Seventy-three _____

Sharing is the art of giving no less,
yet the desire of taking no more.

In all of ❀ her honesty,
She is woman, She is beauty.

_____ Seventy-five _____

As I watch the playful little
butterflies fluttering through the
air, in the contentment of my heart
lies reflections of our all. I
have come to understand that although
sometimes it seems as
though two people are forever changing
like the hands of time, it is only because
the essence of who they truly are is
becoming ever more defined.

_____ Seventy-six _____

*Recognizing a person for what they have become is simply a matter of seeing them for who they are.*

*Her joy is as certain as a morning sunrise.*

As I sit beside a flowing fountain
with a teardrop of joy resting in the
softness of my eyes,
all at once the blending of our
hearts speak of those things so special.
Words cannot express my gratitude when
I think about those times I asked
God to send a girl who in all her
unconditional love would always be my friend.

Two hearts meet as strangers:
in time, they become acquaintances:
in love, they become friends.

*Her happiness is displayed in the*

*simplest ways.*

As I give her a fresh white rose
as an expression of our affection, I reflect
on all things pure. I am intent on always doing
my part in the warmth of adoring her,
in the fullness of romancing her most gentle
heart.

_____ Eighty-two_____

*Sometimes the smallest gifts of thoughtfulness are often the greatest acts of love.*

She is to ✿ be adored.

As I slightly place a heart-shaped
locket in the palm of her hand, its
pristine beauty will forever symbolize two hearts
experiencing something that is never too great
nor never too small, simply love, a genuine
gift shared by so few, yet one whose hope
is meant for all.

_____ *Eighty-five* _____

*A heart that seeks to understand love will never find its meaning to be misunderstood.*

*Her friendship is special for the right reasons.*

As I write these touching words I
believe that they will forever express
the meaningful emotions of my heart:
"Sweetness, I'm so thankful for this much
I know to be true that if I could not love me
then I could never truly love you."

*A person can never offer a greater love to another that they have yet to offer unto themselves.*

_____ *Eighty-nine* _____

In all of ✿ her caring,
She is woman, She is beauty.

As I patiently take hold of her into the safety
of my arms feeling the sounds of
her beating heart, in all importance this is my
most compelling prayer whose beauty I
hope that she will always understand:
when love is present in the heart, gentle
is the man.

Love rest in the hope of two hearts
while togetherness lies in the fulfillment
of its promise.

Ninety-two

*Nothing is better than giving her your very best.*

As I draw her portrait with its
many different shades, I know that
in all ways we are the canvas as love
is the art, for what we create as one
is the greatest expression of unity--
a masterpiece of our hearts.

_____ Ninety-four _____

*Love carries forth a clear image
that becomes apparent in the realness of a heart's
appearance.*

_____ *Ninety-five*_____

*Her value is never compromised.*

As I sit on a rolling hilltop
overlooking the scenic landscape of a
late Autumn day, in the willingness of
my heart I embrace her as truly one
of a kind. In something so personal I make a
lifetime promise that though sometimes
she will be out of sight she will never be
out of mind.

Closeness is not merely measured
by what two hearts share while together,
but that which they continue to share
even while apart.

*She is to ❀ be comforted.*

As I admire the peacefulness of a colorful
rainbow left behind by the light
April showers, it is no secret that she is
the lady of my dreams. As the depth of my love for
her grows, though some may see a simple flower
I will always see a lovely rose.

_____ One Hundred _____

*Love presents itself as beautiful because all things beautiful in the heart are present in love.*

In all of ❀ her cheerfulness,
She is woman, She is beauty.

As I glance through the pages in my journal,
the sincerity of words once written speak
much of her dedication. They also reveal
that our hearts, having held on so true,
is a meaningful lesson love will always
teach: the essence of togetherness is never
truly beyond a heart's reach.

Love, if it is to be realized, it must first be given, for the heart can never capture that which it has never truly set free.

In her littlest dream...

in her most simple prayer...

lies her greatest hope...

to be loved always:

As woman, As beauty.

Printed by BoD™in Norderstedt, Germany